PUFFIN BOOKS

The Werepuppy on Holiday

Jacqueline Wilson writes for children of all ages. *The Suitcase Kid* won the Children's Book Award, *Double Act* won the Smarties Prize, *The Illustrated Mum* won the Guardian Children's Book of the Year Award, *Lizzie Zipmouth* won the Gold Smarties Prize and *Girls in Tears* was named the Children's Book of the Year at the 2003 British Book Awards.

Jacqueline lives near London in a house full of over 10,000 books.

JACQUELINE WILSON

The Werepuppy on Holiday

Illustrated by Janet Robertson

PUFFIN

For Kerry-Anne Kirton and Amy Hammel

PUFFIN BOOKS

Published by the Penguin Group
Penguin Books Ltd, 80 Strand, London WC2R 0RL, England
Penguin Group (USA) Inc., 375 Hudson Street, New York, New York 10014, USA
Penguin Group (Canada), 90 Eglinton Avenue East, Suite 700, Toronto, Ontario, Canada M4P 2Y3
(a division of Pearson Penguin Canada Inc.)
Penguin Ireland, 25 St Stephen's Green, Dublin 2, Ireland (a division of Penguin Books Ltd)
Penguin Group (Australia), 250 Camberwell Road, Camberwell, Victoria 3124, Australia
(a division of Pearson Australia Group Pty Ltd)
Penguin Books India Pvt Ltd, 11 Community Centre, Panchsheel Park, New Delhi – 110 017, India
Penguin Group (NZ), 67 Apollo Drive, Rosedale, North Shore 0632, New Zealand
(a division of Pearson New Zealand Ltd)
Penguin Books (South Africa) (Pty) Ltd, 24 Sturdee Avenue, Rosebank,
Johannesburg 2196, South Africa

Penguin Books Ltd, Registered Offices: 80 Strand, London WC2R 0RL, England

penguin.com

First published by Blackie 1994
Published in Puffin Books 1995
Published in this edition 2007
This edition published exclusively for Nestlé breakfast cereals
1

Text copyright © Jacqueline Wilson, 1994
Illustrations copyright © Janet Robertson, 1994
All rights reserved

The moral right of the author and illustrator has been asserted

Made and printed in England by Clays Ltd, St Ives plc

British Library Cataloguing in Publication Data
A CIP catalogue record for this book is available from the British Library

ISBN: 978-0-141-32314-5

1 . . .

'Right, everyone,' said Miss Monk. 'Time to start clearing out your desks ready for the summer holidays.'

Micky hummed happily as he scrabbled through the mini municipal rubbish dump inside his desk. He kept coming across long forgotten treasures underneath his school books and drawings and scribbled notes. And there was the yellow ochre that had gone missing from his best box of coloured crayons! He hadn't been able to do a proper portrait of his pet, Wolfie, for weeks. Micky found a half-chewed Mars bar that had only gone a little mangy at the edges. He munched appreciatively as he riffled through his drawings, colouring in Wolfie's yellow eyes. Each newly crayoned pair of eyes glowed at him gratefully.

'Micky?' said Miss Monk. 'What are you up to?'

Micky jumped, swallowed the last morsel of Mars, and choked.

Darren Smith leant forward and thumped Micky on the back, much harder than was necessary.

Micky coughed and spluttered, practically knocked head-first into his open desk by Darren's assault.

Micky and Darren Smith were Deadly Enemies.

'All right, Darren, that will do!' said Miss Monk.

'But he's choking, Miss. I'm helping him, Miss. That's what you do when someone chokes, you thump them on the back like this, see.' Darren demonstrated vigorously.

'Darren! Stop it. You get on with tidying up your own desk,' said Miss Monk, walking over to them. 'OK now, Micky?'

'Mmm,' Micky mumbled, sitting up straight.

He stopped choking but he was still bright red in the face. He adored Miss Monk with a devotion that was almost painful. She looked especially lovely today in her blue summer dress and her long black hair tucked back behind one ear with a little bluebird slide.

Micky didn't know how he was going to stand

not being in Miss Monk's class after the summer holidays. He was going to miss her so much. He wished he had a present to give her. He'd given twenty pence to bossy Judy the form monitor when she went round collecting and she had given Miss Monk a big bunch of flowers, but that was from everyone.

Micky fumbled in the depths of his desk, hoping that he might find another Mars bar, preferably unchewed, to give to Miss Monk.

She was peering at Micky's chocolatey mouth, eyebrows raised.

'Have you been eating in class, Micky?' she said.

'Why do you think he was choking, eh, Miss?' Darren hissed. 'Eating gungy old chocolate that's been mouldering in his desk for months. It's probably all gone rancid and poisonous by now and he'll be sick any minute.'

'You mind your own business, Darren,' said Miss Monk. 'And you stop eating all your old forgotten snacks, Micky, and get on with tidying your desk. No more drawing either – not just now.'

Miss Monk tried to sound stern but her mouth was all smiley round the edges. She bent forward, her shiny black hair brushing Micky's cheek, her lovely lilac smell making his nostrils twitch.

'You really are good at drawing, Micky,' said Miss Monk, smiling properly at his pictures.

Micky suddenly had a brilliant idea.

'Would you like to pick one as a goodbye present, Miss Monk?' he suggested.

7

'Oh Micky. That's a lovely idea,' said Miss Monk.

She picked out a picture of Micky running along with Wolfie. Wolfie was on his lead but he was way in front, pulling Micky along. Wolfie generally took charge of Micky when they were out. When they were in too, as a matter of fact.

'I'd like this one, Micky, if that's really all right,' said Miss Monk. 'I'll pin it up in my flat and then I'll always think of you when I look at it.'

Micky went redder than ever, this time with pride.

'Here, Miss, how about having one of my pictures?' said Darren, offering her a whole sheath of scribbles. 'So you can remember me too, eh?'

'I think I'll always remember you, Darren,' said Miss Monk, laughing. She stretched and rubbed the back of her neck. 'It's been quite a busy term one way and another. I'm looking forward to the holidays.'

'Me too, Miss. We're going to Florida,' said Darren proudly. 'To Disneyland.' He leant forward and gave Micky another poke in the back. 'To see Micky Mouse.'

Micky wriggled away from Darren's sharp finger. Darren and all his gang were forever calling him Micky Mouse. It got on Micky's nerves. He did his best to ignore Darren and got on with sorting his drawings. He stroked the shiny crayon portrait of Wolfie with one finger.

The other children were all chatting excitedly

about their summer holidays. Two of the girls were also going to Disneyland, and one boy was going to EuroDisney in France. There were going to be a lot of people wearing Micky Mouse ears during the summer.

Some of the children were going to Spain and some were going to Greece. One girl was going to Cornwall, one boy was going to Blackpool. Several children were going to stay with their gran or their aunty, and bossy Judy was going on a special summer camp in the country.

'Where are you going, Micky?' asked Miss Monk.

'We're not going anywhere,' said Micky.

Micky was part of a big family. Much *too* big, Micky often thought. He had three elder sisters, Meryl and Mandy and Mona. Then he had a little sister, Marigold, and she was a right pain. Mum was OK but Dad could get ever so cross and tetchy at times. Especially nowadays, as the firm he worked for was nearly going bust and Dad was worried he might lose his job. He'd had to take a cut in his wages already.

'We can't afford to go on holiday this year,' said Micky.

'Oh Micky, I'm sorry,' said Miss Monk.

'I don't mind, honestly,' said Micky. And he didn't. He was desperately looking forward to six long weeks at home with Wolfie.

Micky loved Wolfie more than anyone. Even Miss Monk. And yet not so long ago Micky had been terrified of all dogs, even the silliest, squattest old lady's corgi. That's why Mum had taken him to Webb's Dog Shelter to pick out a puppy.

She had felt it was the best way to cure Micky of his fear of dogs.

Micky hadn't been at all keen on the puppy idea. But then he had spotted Wolfie, a strange mangy grey pup, very wild and whiney and bad-tempered. Marigold had tried to pat him and Wolfie had practically chewed her finger off. Micky had taken to Wolfie in a big way after that.

Micky was the only one who realized the most amazing thing about this weird little puppy. He had watched *Savage Snarl*, the famously scary film about werewolves. Wolfie wasn't a puppy-*dog*. He was a baby werewolf. A werepuppy.

That was why Wolfie got into so much trouble and simply refused to be properly trained. He couldn't *help* creating havoc. He terrorized half the neighbourhood and Micky's mum and dad were forever threatening to send him back to the dog shelter. Micky knew he'd have to take Wolfie properly in hand this summer. (And Wolfie thought he'd have to take Micky properly in paw.)

'I'm going to have a smashing summer, Miss Monk,' said Micky. 'I'm going to take Wolfie to the park every day.'

The last time Micky had taken him to the park, Wolfie had picked a fight with every dog in sight, barked hysterically at the ducks on the pond, and snatched an ice-cream from a small child's hand and swallowed it in one gulp. The ice-cream, not the hand. Wolfie was actually quite gentle with most little children. Apart from Marigold.

'I'm going to spend the summer getting Wolfie to obey all my orders,' said Micky, with unreasonable optimism.

Mum brought Wolfie with her when she came to meet Micky and Marigold when school broke up. Wolfie came flying across the playground, his teeth bared in a great grin, his grey fur sticking up spikily.

Most of the children laughed and pointed. Some

stepped back rather rapidly out of Wolfie's way. Darren Smith just happened to be bending down, doing up his Doc Martens. Wolfie spotted him and his grin grew wider. He decided to try out a goat imitation. He lowered his head and charged. Wolfie butted Darren right on the bottom and sent him flying.

Darren wasn't hurt. Just his dignity. Everyone laughed at him. Micky practically fell about, and Wolfie gave short sharp barks as if he was snorting with laughter too.

Darren didn't find it funny at all.

'That mangy old dog ought to be put down!' he yelled. 'You keep it away from me, Micky.'

'I think it's certainly about time you got your dog trained, Micky,' said Miss Monk, crossing the playground.

'He can be good sometimes, honestly, Miss,' said Micky.

And as if to prove his point Wolfie wiped his paws on the sprawling Darren Smith and trotted meekly up to Miss Monk, head a little bowed, as if overcome by her presence.

'Say hallo to Miss Monk, Wolfie,' said Micky.

Wolfie raised one paw very politely, and Miss Monk laughed and shook hands.

'You're certainly going to keep each other busy during the holidays,' she said. 'Have a lovely time anyway, Micky. And thank you again for the picture.'

Micky danced home in a dream, and Wolfie

seemed a little dazed too. He kept bumping into Marigold.

'Get *off* me,' Marigold whined. 'Mum, he's slavering all over me, yuck! It's not *fair*. How come Micky can have Wolfie when I haven't got a pet? When am I going to get a pony, eh? I've wanted one for ages and ages, and it wouldn't have to cost all that much. I could feed it grass and dandelions and that and – '

'Oh, Marigold, do give it a rest,' said Mum.

'My friend Fiona's going pony-trekking this summer, Mum. Can I at least go pony-trekking? Oh please.'

'I'm sorry, Marigold, but I really don't think we can manage it. We just can't have any proper holiday this year,' said Mum, sighing. She sounded as if she certainly needed a holiday.

'It's not *fair*,' said Marigold all the way home.

When Meryl and Mandy and Mona got home from school they too were all agreed that it wasn't fair. Meryl wanted to go to Spain to sunbathe in her new bikini. Mandy wanted to go to Wales to walk for miles in the mountains. Mona's best friend was another one going to Disneyland and Mona moaned and moaned and moaned because she couldn't go too.

'Put a sock in it, Mona,' Micky muttered.

Wolfie thought Micky had issued a command and went off searching, coming back a few minutes later with one of Dad's socks which he'd got out of the laundry basket. He'd laundered it himself with all his slaver. Dad was not going to be pleased. Wolfie's teeth were sharp and the sock had several holes that were going to take quite a lot of darning.

Micky quickly shoved the sock back in the laundry basket. Dad was usually so bad-tempered when he came home from work that seeing a perforated sock might well make him explode. Micky gave Wolfie a bone to keep him reasonably quiet and settled down to do another drawing.

'I'm making up a place called Mickyland,' he muttered to Wolfie. 'It's like Disneyland only better, and no-one else can go there. It's just for you and me, Wolfie. We've got all the rides to ourselves and we don't ever have to queue, and we can eat ice-creams all day long. That would be good, eh?'

Wolfie thumped his tail, agreeing that it would be very good indeed.

2 . . .

Dad was very late home from work.

'Oh dear,' said Mum. 'I hope he's all right. Well, we'd better have tea without him.'

Mum put Dad's cottage pie on one side, ready to pop in the microwave when he came home, and dished up everybody else's meal.

The girls were still talking about holidays. Or the lack of them.

'Don't go on like this when Dad gets home,' said Mum anxiously. 'Eat up your tea, come on. And Micky, stop messing about with your food.'

Micky was busy turning his cottage pie into a real cottage, with carrots for windows and a green courgette front door. He had already tiled the roof with his fork and supported the sagging walls with his knife. He'd made such a perfect cottage that it seemed a shame to eat it.

'*Micky!*'

Micky ate. When he got to the boring sloshy bit under the crisp potato he snapped his fingers for Wolfie to come and help him out.

But Wolfie wasn't there.

'Wolfie? Wolfie?' Micky called.

'Finish your tea, Micky,' said Mum.

But Micky was cocking one ear at the kitchen, all systems alert. He heard a distant enthusiastic

15

chomping.

'Oh no,' said Micky, rushing to the kitchen.

Wolfie was finishing *his* tea. Only it wasn't really Wolfie's tea. It was Dad's.

'Oh no! What am I going to give your dad for his tea now?' said Mum. 'I'm not doing my big shop till tomorrow. There's nothing in the fridge. Oh Wolfie, you *bad* dog.'

'I'm sorry, Mum,' said Micky. 'And Wolfie's sorry too, aren't you, Wolfie?'

Wolfie didn't look a bit sorry. He was licking his lips appreciatively, obviously very partial to cottage pie.

'Dad can have the rest of my cottage pie, Mum,' Micky offered.

But Micky's cottage pie was now demolis[...] rubble and it did not look appetizing.

Micky decided it might be wise to get Wolfie out of the way before Dad came home. Mandy had already finished her veggieburger (she did her own cooking now she was a vegetarian) and was busy packing newspapers into Mum's shopping trolley. Mandy delivered the local paper one evening a week to earn some pocket money.

'I'll help you with your deliveries,' said Micky. 'And Wolfie will too. He can carry some of the newspapers in his mouth.'

'These newspapers have to be delivered in pristine condition – not soggy shreds after your carnivore has slobbered all over them,' said Mandy.

Micky sighed. Mandy was still his favourite sister, but only just. Now she didn't eat meat she seemed to have an awful down on Wolfie, who ate little else. An unfortunate encounter between Wolfie and Wilbur, Mandy's pet white rat, hadn't helped either.

Mandy had let Wilbur have a little walkabout in her bedroom. Wolfie had come barging in, nose aquiver, and spotted a walking white sausage with a tail. Wolfie had followed his instincts and there was very nearly a terrible tragic accident. Luckily, Micky had managed to prise Wolfie's mouth open and Mandy managed to nurse poor Wilbur back to full health, though he'd been understandably twitchy ever since.

'Go on, Mandy, we want to help you,' said Micky.

'No way,' said Mandy.

'Oh, let them come with you, Mandy,' said Mum. She could see that it might be better to keep Micky and Wolfie out of Dad's way. 'I worry about you going round the streets on your own. Wolfie will be protection for you.'

'Ha!' said Mandy. '*I* need to be protected from Wolfie.'

But she gave in and let them trot round delivering too. Wolfie did his best to be well behaved at first, though he couldn't quite get the hang of all the stopping and starting while they delivered the newspapers. He kept bounding forwards, thinking they were going walkies, and Micky had to dig in his heels and haul him back each time.

When they eventually got to the end of the road and turned the corner they saw a gang of boys from Mandy's secondary school.

'Oh-oh. Trouble,' said Mandy, squaring her shoulders.

They were the sort of boys who made Darren Smith and his gang look like *Blue Peter* boy scouts.

'Hey look, it's old Milly-Molly-Mandy with her kid brother and some dopey mongrel pup,' said one of the boys. 'Out delivering newspapers. Aaah, isn't that sweet? Like us to help you, Mandy?'

'No thanks,' said Mandy, trying to march straight past. 'Come on, Micky.'

But the boys were blocking their way.

'That's not very nice of you, Mandy. Why can't we help you, eh? You'll get it done much quicker if we all lend a hand. So give us the papers, right?'

It wasn't right at all. The boys were grabbing newspapers out of the shopping trolley and throwing them wildly to each other. Papers flapped through the air like unwieldy birds and then flopped to the ground, all their pages crumpling.

'You stop that,' said Mandy.

'Yes, stop it,' said Micky.

'Woof,' said Wolfie, getting excited, chasing after the papers as if it was a great game.

The boys laughed and went on throwing. Mandy tried to grab some of the newspapers back and the biggest boy elbowed her out of the way.

Mandy staggered and tried to push back and the boy shoved his hand in her face.

'Don't you hit my sister!' Micky shouted, and he hurled himself at the boy, trying to rugby tackle him round the waist. The big boy kicked backwards and Micky found himself on the pavement. The boy still had hold of Mandy, hurting her.

Micky was boiling with rage, itching and aching, clenched ready to make a further attack.

But he didn't have to. Someone else went to the rescue. Wolfie stopped savaging a newspaper, saw Micky on the pavement, Mandy struggling with the boy, and growled. His fur stood up and he seemed to grow before their eyes. He was still only a puppy but somehow he seemed transformed, a huge hairy savage creature with wild eyes and bared teeth.

He sprang in the air and pounced on the boy, who gave a high-pitched scream and shot forwards, leaving the entire seat of his jeans in Wolfie's jaws.

'He bit my bum! He bit my bum!' the boy yelled, running like mad.

Wolfie growled triumphantly, eyeing the other boys, obviously revving up for a further attack. They decided to beat a hasty retreat. They all went flying down the road, Wolfie chasing after them for the pure fun of it.

'Good boy, Wolfie!' Micky yelled delightedly. 'See, Mandy. Wolfie did protect you, didn't he? You can't still be cross with him now.'

'OK, OK,' said Mandy, giving Micky a quick

hug. 'You all right, little pal? Those thugs didn't hurt you, did they?'

'No, but they hurt you, didn't they? You're going to need Wolfie and me to protect you every delivery day now, isn't that right?'

'Yeah. Well. Maybe,' said Mandy, brushing herself down and grinning. 'Here, Wolfie! Here boy! Come and get thanked.'

Wolfie lolloped back, chomping on the jeans as if they were chewing-gum. He pranced in front of Mandy, letting her pat and praise him profusely, his amber eyes glistening.

Micky started to gather up the crumpled newspapers and Wolfie tried to help. He'd got so over-excited now that he scattered the papers further, and chewed the few he did collect into soggy pulp.

'Wolfie! *No*, boy. Here, leave off,' said Mandy, but she couldn't get cross again.

Micky tried to piece all the floating parts together, but as Wolfie had chewed the edges where the page numbers were it was a very hard job. There was a colouring competition on the children's page which caught his eye, a seaside scene. He'd maybe have a go at colouring it in now he had a yellow crayon for the sand. There were seaside adverts on the opposite page, including a special last-minute deal for a week in a big hotel on the south coast cliffs. The Amber Hotel. There was a blurry photo of it, too. Micky decided to colour the roof and doors and windows yellow when he was going in for the competition.

It was almost dark by the time Mandy and Micky and Wolfie got home.

Mum was looking out for them.

'There you are! I was getting really worried. First Dad goes missing, and then you three.'

'Dad's back then?' said Micky, wondering if he and Wolfie should make themselves scarce again.

'Yes,' said Mum, but she was smiling now. 'He was late because his boss took him for a drink.'

'Dad hasn't lost his job, has he, Mum?' said Mandy.

'No, thank goodness. Things have picked up at his work. They've got a new order in. The boss is very pleased with your dad,' said Mum, obviously enormously relieved.

Dad was sitting at the kitchen table eating fish and chips. Marigold was on his lap, scrounging chips from his plate.

'I hear Wolfie helped himself to my tea,' said Dad, but he was smiling.

'Sorry, Dad,' said Micky. He nudged Wolfie, to try to make him look sorry too.

Dad laughed. 'Oh well. As long as I don't have to go and fetch myself fish and chips *every* teatime. Anyway, things are looking up, chaps. My boss was even hinting at a wage rise. So we could maybe have had a bit of a holiday after all. Still, I suppose everywhere will be booked up now.'

'Hey, I know where we could go,' said Micky. He delved into Mandy's shopping bag amongst the

totally chewed-up leftover papers and tried to piece one together. 'Here it is! Look – the Amber Hotel. A week's bargain break.'

'Couldn't we go on a week's bargain break to Disneyland?' said Marigold.

'You never give up, do you, pet?' said Dad, feeding her another chip. 'No, we can't quite make it to Disneyland – but let's have a look at this hotel deal, Micky.'

'Oh, I love that bit of the coast,' said Mum, reading the advert too. 'Do you think we could really afford it? Tell you what. My mum could come on holiday with us. She could really do with a bit of sea air after that bout of bronchitis.'

'Oh great! Can Granny Boot really come too?' said Micky, who adored his gran.

'Mmm,' said Dad, not sounding at all sure he liked the idea. He was nowhere near as fond of Granny Boot as Micky was.

'Then she could always babysit for us in the evenings,' said Mum, wheedling a little.

'Ah. Yes. Well, OK then,' said Dad. 'So we'd need . . . three rooms. One for us. One for Meryl and Mandy and Mona. And then Granny Boot can share with Micky and Marigold.'

'And Wolfie,' said Micky.

There was a sudden silence.

'What about Wolfie?' Micky repeated.

Wolfie barked insistently, as if he was asking the same question.

3 . . .

Micky couldn't believe it.

'What do you *mean*?' he shouted. 'Wolfie's *got* to come too! I can't go on holiday without Wolfie.'

'Come on now, Micky, calm down,' said Mum.

'If you keep shouting like that you won't be going on any holiday,' said Dad.

'I don't want to go on holiday – not without Wolfie,' Micky yelled.

'Good,' said Marigold. 'We'll leave you and Wolfie at home.'

'We *can't* leave Wolfie,' said Micky, getting desperate.

'Micky's going to cry in a minute,' said Marigold. 'Look, he's getting all red in the face. *Baby!*'

Micky got even redder, boiling with rage. Yes, there were tears in his eyes, but it was because he was so angry. He couldn't understand his family. How could they possibly be so mean? They all seemed *happy* with the idea of a holiday without Wolfie.

Wolfie was becoming upset too, bounding from one to another, looking for reassurance.

'Get off me, Wolfie. I don't want your mangy old dog hairs all over my new skirt,' Meryl fussed.

'*Down*, Wolfie,' Mandy commanded, because

she was giving Wilbur rat a little ride on her shoulder.

'Yuck, Wolfie's slobbered all over me,' Mona moaned.

'Wolfie's going for me now! Get him off me! Help help help,' Marigold whimpered affectedly, waving her arms about. One of her fingers caught Wolfie on his soft snout, scratching him. He growled indignantly – and Marigold squealed and squirmed.

'Help, Dad! He's going to bite!'

'I hope he does. I hope he bites you all – because you're all so horrible not letting him come on holiday,' Micky shouted.

Wolfie growled louder in agreement, and ever so slightly nipped one of Marigold's fat little fingers.

Wolfie ended up banished to the garden where he howled miserably.

Micky ended up banished to his bedroom. He howled too. He couldn't believe how quickly

everything had gone wrong, the holidays spoiled before they'd even got started. And it made it even worse knowing that it was his own fault. He was the one who'd read about the wretched hotel. *He'd* suggested it.

'Oh Micky, don't take on so,' said Mum, coming into his room. 'Look, maybe you're getting into a state about nothing. Perhaps this Amber Hotel will let dogs stay too. There are a few hotels that don't mind pets. Although Wolfie's so wild I'm not sure anyone would welcome *him*.'

'I would,' Micky snuffled. 'And he can't help being a bit wild, Mum. It's the way he was born. He's . . . he's not like other dogs.'

'You can say that again,' said Mum.

She did her best for Wolfie, though. She phoned up the Amber Hotel. Yes, their bargain offer was still open. Yes, they had three family rooms available. Yes, they'd be delighted to accept their booking. Pets? Ah. A puppy. Mmm. Sorry. No.

'We wouldn't bring him into the hotel,' Mum tried. 'We could keep him in the garden. We'd try our hardest not to let him be a nuisance. It's just my son adores his puppy and it will spoil his entire holiday if they're separated . . . '

But it was no use. The hotel said they really couldn't take pets as well as people.

Mum sighed and said sorry to Micky.

'We can't go then?' said Micky, refusing to give up.

'We all need a holiday, Micky,' said Mum.

28

'*Wolfie* needs a holiday,' said Micky.

'Well, he can *have* a holiday,' said Mum. 'He can go back to Webb's Dog Shelter for the week. He'll like that, Micky. He can meet up with all his doggy pals again.'

Wolfie's howls increased dramatically out in the garden. He didn't sound as if he liked that idea at all.

'Micky! Where are you, boy? Come down here at once,' Dad shouted, forgetting that he was the one who had banished Micky to the bedroom. 'Get that dog of yours under control, do you hear me? If he doesn't quit that row he'll be staying at Webb's Dog Shelter for good.'

Micky saw it was wiser not to argue with Dad right at the present moment. He hurtled out into the garden. Wolfie was rampaging up and down, tossing his head, growling and groaning, howling and moaning.

'Oh poor Wolfie!' said Micky, trying to catch him.

'Shut him up, Micky,' said Meryl, coming out into the garden to feed her rabbits. 'Here, Rachel, Roberta. Din-dins,' she said, waving a handful of dandelions in the direction of their hutch.

Rachel and Roberta were cowering in a corner, convinced by Wolfie's savage howls that *they* were din-dins.

'Poor little things,' said Meryl. 'Honestly, Micky, you've got to get Wolfie under control. He's scaring them silly.'

'Hey, what about Rachel and Roberta?' Micky said, flinging himself on his much maligned pet. 'Who's going to look after them if we go on this horrid old holiday? You don't get rabbit shelters, do you?'

Wolfie threw back his head and howled hungrily, as if he could solve the Rachel and Roberta rabbit problem at one fell swoop.

Mrs Charlton next door said that she wouldn't mind popping over the garden fence to feed Meryl's rabbits. She said she could cope with Wilbur rat too, as long as he would keep to his cage.

'So could you look after my Wolfie too?' Micky asked hopefully. He still couldn't bear the thought of parting from his werepuppy, but he knew Wolfie would be much happier in his own home than shut up in the dog shelter.

Mrs Charlton was very kind, but there was a limit to her neighbourliness.

'I'm not going near that dog,' she said firmly. 'Not even if *he's* put in a cage like the rat. And while we're on the subject of the dog, I wish you'd find some way of stopping him howling. It makes all the hairs stand up on the back of my neck. The noise he makes at night – especially when there's a full moon!'

Micky saw there was no point trying to persuade Mrs Charlton. Her mind was made up.

Mum and Dad's minds were made up too. And Meryl's and Mandy's and Mona's and Marigold's. They all wanted to go on their bumper bargain break holiday at the Amber Hotel – and it was just Wolfie's hard luck that he couldn't go too.

Granny Boot was delighted to be asked on holiday with the family. Mum rang her up that evening and Granny came rushing round on Saturday, after she'd cruised round one car boot sale, a boy scout's jumble, and half a dozen charity shops. Her shopping trolley was full of fifties flowery frocks and sixties miniskirts and seventies crochet and patchwork, treasures for her own second-hand clothes shop. Meryl delved through the pile of clothes eagerly, because she was very into seventies fashion. Mandy wasn't into any kind of fashion at all, but Granny Boot had found an almost new pair of football boots in Mandy's size, so she was thrilled.

'Haven't you got anything for me, Gran?' Mona moaned, but she perked up considerably when Granny Boot produced a bright pink Speedo swimming costume. Mona had recently learnt to swim and was already flashing up and down the local pool.

'And look, Marigold, I got you this dinky little bikini,' said Granny. 'You'll look ever so cute in it, pet. You can wear it on the beach on holiday, eh? Oooh, won't it be fun?'

Granny Boot laughed enthusiastically and then coughed and spluttered.

'Here, Micky, pat us on the back, there's a good little chap,' Granny gasped.

'You're still ever so wheezy. Let's hope the sea

31

air does your chest good,' said Mum, giving Granny Boot a cup of tea.

'Thanks, dearie. Well, it's certainly been ages since I had a proper holiday, what with the shop and that. Still, my friend Monica says she'll look after it for me.' Granny sipped her tea, looking at Micky.

'What's up with my little pal, eh? Did you think your old gran has given some goodies to all your sisters and forgotten you?' Granny laughed and coughed all over again. 'Here, Micky. Look, what's this, eh?'

She held out a very smart blue and silver dog lead.

'Thank you, Gran,' said Micky in a very small voice.

'Oooh dear, there's still something the matter, isn't there? Oh goodness, it's not your Wolfie? He's all right?'

There was a sudden angry shouting and anguished barking from the bathroom upstairs. Wolfie had been nosing in the laundry basket for Dad's other sock to make a matching perforated pair, and Dad had caught him in mid-chew.

Wolfie came flying down the stairs and into the kitchen, hurling himself into Micky's arms.

'Well, he looks in fine fettle to me,' said Granny, chuckling croakily. She patted Wolfie fondly, scratching him behind the ears. 'Who's been a naughty boy, mmm? What's this hanging out your mouth? Oooh, a sock, is it? That's asking for trouble! Big Daddy up in the bathroom sounds pretty peeved. You'd better hustle Wolfie out the way, Micky, or he'll get punished.'

'He's going to be punished already,' said Micky mournfully. 'They won't let him go on holiday, Gran. They say he's got to go in the dog shelter. He hated it there. He was howling when I first found him.'

'Oh Micky, Wolfie's been howling on and off ever since,' said Mum. 'And it's a lovely dog shelter, ever so clean and all the dogs are well cared for. Miss Webb might even get Wolfie properly trained while he's there.'

'Wolfie doesn't *like* being clean and well cared for and trained,' said Micky. 'He'll think he's in prison.'

'Micky's going to cry again!' Marigold announced scornfully.

'Aren't you going to try on your bikini, Goldilocks?' said Granny Boot. 'Come on, girls, I want a fashion parade.'

While their attention was diverted Granny dabbed at Micky's eyes with an old headscarf and then hauled him up on to her lap, Wolfie on top.

'Watch out, Mum, they'll squash you,' said Micky's mum.

'I fancy a cuddle with my two big bad boys,' said Granny Boot, hugging them hard. 'Yes, I can see it's going to be hard for you two chaps to be separated. Your silly old Gran didn't even think of that.'

Micky sniffed and snuggled in tight to Gran. Wolfie snuffled and squirmed a little, but he was happy to be held too. Granny Boot fumbled for her handbag and found a packet of chocolate toffees. She popped one into her own mouth, one into Micky's, and one into Wolfie's.

Micky managed a small smile and Wolfie gave Granny Boot a very chocolatey lick.

'There now. Wolfie and I get on fine together, don't we, young Micky. So tell you what! Will you stop fretting if Wolfie comes to stay with me while you go on your holiday?'

'But you're coming on holiday too, Gran.'

'I'm not so sure it's such a good idea, pet. I don't like to leave my shop. My friend Monica minds it for me on Saturdays, yes, but I'm not sure she can manage a whole week. No, I'll stay home and Wolfie can stay with me. Yes? So you can cheer up right this minute, little pal.'

Micky was very touched but troubled. Wolfie would much sooner stay with Gran than go to Webb's Dog Shelter – but Micky wanted Gran to go on holiday with him. Micky wanted Gran *and* Wolfie to go on holiday with him. But that wasn't possible, so . . .

'Can I stay with you too, Gran?' said Micky. 'Us three could all have a sort-of holiday at home.'

'You're a caution, Micky,' said Gran, laughing and then coughing again.

'Oh Mum,' said Micky's mum. 'Off your gran, Micky, you and Wolfie really are too heavy for her. Now listen, you three. Granny badly needs a holiday by the sea to shake off the last of her bronchitis. And you need a holiday by the sea, young Micky, because you're getting all pale and peevish and it will do you the world of good. And Wolfie needs a short sharp spell in Webb's Dog Shelter to get him licked into shape.'

'But, Mum – '

'No buts. That's what's going to happen, whether you like it or not.'

Micky didn't like it at all. But when Mum spoke in that tone of voice he knew there was no point arguing.

4 . . .

The family were all packed and in the car. It had taken hours and hours for them to get to this stage. Meryl had wanted to take two huge suitcases crammed with the entire contents of her wardrobe. Mandy had promised to do her own packing too and had simply shoved a spare pair of jeans and a couple of T-shirts in a carrier bag. Mum had had to waste a lot of time persuading Mandy to take more and Meryl a lot less. Mona moaned all the time that she didn't have any nice new clothes and it wasn't fair. Micky didn't care about clothes, old or new, but he was in such a state over parting with Wolfie that he kept dissolving into tears. Wolfie couldn't understand why and kept licking Micky's salty cheeks affectionately.

'Yuck, how can you stand to have him slobbering all over you like that?' said Marigold, trying to squeeze all six of her Little Ponies *and* their stable into her suitcase. 'And why do you keep blubbering like a baby, Micky? Your stupid big bad wolf looks thrilled to bits to be going back to the dog shelter.'

'Shut up,' said Micky. 'He doesn't realize properly. He thinks he's going on holiday with us.'

Micky hadn't bothered with his own packing but he'd sorted out Wolfie's new lead and his favourite blanket and bone. Wolfie had watched with interest, bounding about excitedly. Micky felt sick with guilt. He knew he should try to explain to Wolfie but every time he tried to tell him he got all choked up and cried.

He was very nearly crying now as he sat squeezed up beside Granny Boot in the back of the car, Wolfie on his lap.

'For goodness sake, pull yourself together Micky,' said Dad sharply. 'We're going on holiday, not going to a funeral. Now, first stop this dog shelter, right?'

'Oh Dad, please, *please* let Wolfie come on holiday with us. I'm sure if we just turned up with him at the Amber Hotel and they saw how cute he is they wouldn't really mind,' Micky said desperately.

'And when he howled all night and disgraced

himself on the carpet and bit the other guests I'm sure they wouldn't really mind that either,' said Dad sarcastically.

'How about if Wolfie stayed in the car then? I could sleep in the car too just to make sure he's all right and – '

'Micky,' said Mum. 'We've been through this a dozen times. Stop it. Wolfie's going into the dog shelter. Now, I can appreciate it's very upsetting for you, so I'll take him in if you like.'

'No. If he's got to stay there then I'll take him,' said Micky. He had his arms tightly round Wolfie, his cheek pressed hard against his head. Wolfie squirmed and whimpered a little, starting to feel uneasy.

Dad drew up outside Webb's Dog Shelter and Wolfie gave a sudden startled yelp.

'Here, Wolfie. A little treat,' said Granny Boot quickly, delving in her handbag. She popped two chocolate toffees in Wolfie's mouth. 'There now. Take him in quickly, Micky.'

Micky gathered up his pet and carried him to the door. Wolfie scrabbled to escape. He sniffed the air, tensed, and then let out a long howl, chocolate drooling down his chin.

'I recognize that howl!' said Miss Webb, opening the door.

Her twin labradors, Rough and Tumble, growled, and little Jeannie the Scottie scuttled out of harm's way. They obviously recognized Wolfie too.

'Shall I take him?' said Miss Webb. 'Here, boy. Remember me?'

Wolfie howled harder. He twisted and turned, scrabbling and scratching Micky desperately, his amber eyes big with betrayal.

'Oh Wolfie, I'm sorry,' said Micky. 'It's not my fault, honest. They won't let you come on holiday with us, and I know it's not fair, and I'd give anything for you to come too. *Please* don't look like that. It's only for a week and then I'll come and get you.'

'Don't worry about him. We'll see he's OK and make a big fuss of him,' said Miss Webb, holding out her arms for Wolfie.

Wolfie stiffened all over and bared his teeth, snarling. He did his best to cling to Micky, practically winding his paws round his neck.

'Oh Wolfie, please, you've got to try and be a good dog,' said Micky, though he knew how unfair it was to expect a baby werewolf to be anything but bad.

He gave Wolfie one last long loving hug and kiss, and Wolfie stopped struggling and snarling for a moment and licked Micky mournfully, coating his cheeks with chocolate.

'Better go now, while he's quiet,' said Miss Webb, taking hold of Wolfie.

The moment she held him Wolfie stopped being quiet. He howled and growled and snarled and snapped, so that Miss Webb had her work cut out holding on to him.

'Here's his blanket and all his bits,' said Micky, giving her the carrier bag. 'And for a special treat he loves chocolate toffees. I'll just run and get another toffee or two from my gran.'

'Well, that's not really very good for his teeth,' said Miss Webb, shaking her head.

Wolfie's teeth certainly seemed in very good shape at the moment. He was doing his best to bite hard.

'Oh Wolfie,' said Micky helplessly. 'You do understand, don't you? I'm not leaving you here for good.'

Wolfie seemed to think Micky was leaving him for bad. He was working himself up into such a state that Micky couldn't bear it. He ran to Granny Boot for a whole handful of chocolate toffees.

'Here, Wolfie,' he said, offering the treat.

Wolfie usually gobbled chocolate toffees in one gulp. But this time he seized just one, holding it in his teeth, looking straight at Micky.

'What is it, Wolfie? You can eat it,' said Micky.

Wolfie didn't swallow. He'd stopped struggling. He stayed still, his eyes bigger than ever, glowing gold, looking straight at Micky.

Micky looked back at Wolfie. He blinked back his tears. Wolfie was saying something, as clearly as if he were speaking. Micky nodded and Wolfie nodded too. Then Wolfie swallowed his chocolate toffee and started chewing Miss Webb's fingers instead – and Micky gave him one last pat and trailed back to the car.

'About time too,' said Dad. 'We're never going to get there today at this rate.'

'Wolfie will be fine, Micky,' said Mum.

'Wolfie will probably be in his element chatting up all the lady dogs,' said Meryl.

'And he'll have fun winning all the dog fights,' said Mandy.

'Isn't it quiet in the car without Wolfie,' said Mona.

'Micky's crying,' said Marigold.

Granny Boot didn't say anything at all, but she passed Micky her hanky and offered him her bag of chocolate toffees when all his sisters were looking the other way. Micky took one. He was hidden behind the big hanky so no one actually saw him eating it.

'Do you mind if we have the window open a bit, Granny?' he asked.

'Of course not, dearie, I like a bit of a blow,' said Granny Boot, winding the window down.

Micky stuck his head half out of the window and let his arm hang out too.

'Sit down properly, you silly boy,' said Dad. 'That's dangerous!'

Micky moped again. Granny Boot offered him another chocolate toffee. And then another. And another.

Micky kept edging up to the open window.

'Are you feeling all right, pet?' Granny Boot whispered.

'I – I feel a bit sick,' Micky mumbled.

'Well, no wonder! You've nearly finished the chocolate toffees, and I had a great big jumbo bag full when we set out!' Granny Boot sounded worried. 'Ooh dear, I shouldn't have let you have so many.'

'You shouldn't have let Micky have so many what?' said Marigold.

'It's not fair,' Mona moaned. 'Granny's been giving Micky toffees and we haven't had any.'

'I want a chocolate toffee!' Marigold demanded.

'Pipe down you lot!' Dad shouted, but he stopped at the next motorway service station and bought a big bag of chocolate toffees for everyone. Micky still claimed his fair share.

'Don't make yourself ill, lovey,' Granny Boot whispered. 'I've never known you eat so many. It's almost as if you were feeding young Wolfie too.'

Micky fidgeted and hung his head.

'He'll be all right, you'll see,' said Granny Boot, putting her arm round him.

'I hope so,' said Micky, snuggling close.

5 . . .

The Amber Hotel looked lovely, with hanging baskets of flowers, tubs of geraniums all round the porch, and honeysuckle and roses climbing up the white walls. The doors and window frames were shiny yellow, as if a giant Micky had just coloured them in with his crayon.

'Doesn't it look wonderful?' said Mum.

'There! We're going to have a great holiday,' said Dad, putting his arm round her.

'It looks ever so friendly and welcoming,' said Granny Boot.

'Not to *some* people,' Micky muttered. 'I'm surprised they haven't got barbed wire round the flowerbeds and notices all over saying DOGS KEEP OUT!'

The lady who owned the hotel was standing in reception all smiles, but Micky glowered at her.

She showed them to their rooms. Mum and Dad seemed very happy with theirs, and Granny Boot loved the old-fashioned furniture, admiring the art deco mirrors and Lloyd Loom chairs, but the girls were less impressed.

'We haven't got an en suite bathroom! I can't go trailing down the corridor in my nightie, someone might *see* me!' said Meryl.

'We haven't got a telly in our room and I wanted

to see a bit of *Grandstand*,' said Mandy.

'No television! How am I going to watch *Neighbours* and *Home and Away*?' Mona wailed.

'And where's the mini-bar?' said Marigold, rushing round the room she was sharing with Micky and Granny Boot. 'All my friends say you get special mini-bars in your room in hotels and you can have all these ice-cold cans of Coke whenever you want. And you get baby bottles of drink, whisky and vodka and gin, and I wanted Dad to drink them so I could have the bottles for my dolls.'

'What's that, pet?' Dad called from his room, determinedly cheery now that he was on holiday. 'Now listen here, you moaning Minnies. This is a lovely old-fashioned family hotel –'

'Only it doesn't cater for *all* the family,' Micky mumbled, flopping on his bed.

'I heard that, Micky,' said Dad, appearing at the door. 'Now stop that silly sulking. And you girls, stop your grouches and show a bit of appreciation. Who wants a new soulless package holiday hotel with blaring tellies and bars?'

'We do,' Mona whispered.

'We're going to have a real traditional family holiday,' said Dad. 'We don't need boring old television. We'll have fun on the beach and play games and soak up the sun – '

'I think it's just started spitting with rain,' Granny Boot said, looking out of the window. 'Oh dear. Those clouds do look black.'

'A spot of rain never hurt anyone,' said Dad, glaring at Granny.

It was more than a spot. It was a downpour. The family finished unpacking and then stood around uncertainly, waiting for the rain to clear up a little.

'I want my lunch, I'm starving,' Marigold complained.

'I'm not,' said Micky, lying on his bed and staring at the wall.

'That's because a certain someone ate a whole bag of chocolate toffees,' said Granny Boot, giving him a pretend pat on the bottom.

'Come on, we'll go and eat,' said Dad, putting on his mac. 'Here, Marigold, there's room for you inside here too.'

He buttoned Marigold up inside his mac and she stepped up on to his feet, giggling.

'Look at the Mac-Monster!' she shouted from

inside. 'Hey, I know what I want to eat. A Big Mac for the Mac-Monster, please!'

Mum was all right in the rain because she had an umbrella and Granny Boot had a plastic rainhood but Micky and his older sisters didn't have hoods or umbrellas. It was only a short walk from the Amber Hotel into the town but they got soaked.

'Honestly, look at my hair!' Meryl complained. 'All the curls gone out, look! I look such a *mess*.'

Mandy always looked a mess and didn't care at all, but she was pretty miserable too, because she was wearing her old plimsolls and they had a hole in each sole.

'Both my feet are going for little private paddles,' she said, her plimsolls squelching at every step.

'It's not fair, why does Marigold get to choose where we eat? I don't want a burger, I want fish and chips,' Mona grumbled.

Micky didn't say a word. He mooched along behind his family, his jumper pulled up over his ears, his chin on his chest.

'Micky, don't pull your jumper out of shape like that,' said Mum. 'Come under my umbrella with me.'

Micky didn't feel like company. He shook his head, scowling.

'You look like a gangster,' said Mum. 'Pull that jumper *down*!'

Micky pulled it down a fraction but kept his neck bent and his shoulders hunched. He wanted to look like a gangster. He curled his hand into a pretend

46

gun, two fingers aiming at his entire family.

'This is a stick-up,' he muttered. 'I'm going to spring my pal Wolfie out of gaol, do you hear me?'

Granny Boot heard and chuckled sympathetically.

'Poor Miss Webb! That dog shelter is a very nice place, Micky. My friend Monica left her poodle there when she went to Majorca and he was ever so perky when she went to fetch him.'

'Yes, but Wolfie isn't a soppy old poodle. He's different,' said Micky.

'I'll say,' said Granny.

'Granny,' said Micky. 'Supposing . . . just supposing Wolfie escaped.'

'No, he couldn't get out, pet, you know that. There are locks on the pens, I'm sure.'

'Yes, but just *supposing*, Granny. Then do you think he could possibly follow my scent and track me down?'

'Oh Micky, don't be daft. We've driven miles and miles and miles. And your Wolfie's only a pup, for all he's getting bigger every day. And even if he was a huge great tracker dog then he couldn't follow your scent because you were in the car, weren't you?'

'So would he just run about looking for me, lost?' said Micky, anxiously. 'Oh Granny, I can't bear to think of him going round and round, calling for me. And he'd be so worried and frightened and so he'd probably be howling and if anyone came near him he'd probably snap a bit because he was feeling miserable and then what if someone thought he was really fierce or even dangerous and called the police and then they caught him and locked him up in one of their cells and . . . and . . .'

'Micky's crying *again*,' announced the Mac-Monster.

Granny Boot passed him her hanky.

'You're going to have to stop moping, pet,' she said. 'You're going to spoil your whole holiday carrying on like this.'

'You're going to spoil *our* holiday,' said Dad. 'Now I'm warning you, Micky. You're going to stop snivelling, buck up and ENJOY yourself! That goes for the lot of you. Meryl, stop going on about your hair, for goodness sake. Mandy, if you'd only wear a decent pair of shoes instead of those disgraceful old plimsolls your feet would stay bone dry. Mona, we'll have fish and chips tomorrow, so stop that silly whining.'

'*I'm* not whining, am I, Dad?' said Marigold smugly. 'Where's the McDonald's then? This Mac-Monster wants feeding *now*.'

But although they walked round the whole town twice, getting wetter and hungrier by the minute, they couldn't find a McDonald's. There weren't any burger bars at all.

'What a lousy rotten swizzle!' said Marigold.

'Look, let's go in the Copper Kettle, it looks really lovely,' said Mum.

'Oooh, home-made steak and kidney pie,' said Granny Boot. 'Bang goes my diet.'

'Roast beef and Yorkshire pudding, mmm,' said Dad.

'Yuck!' said Marigold, stamping on his feet. 'I don't want meat in slices and chunks, I can't eat it like that. I want a Big Mac!'

'Ouch! Stop that silly stamping this minute, Marigold!' said Dad, trying to get her out from under his mac.

'But I want – '

'You'll get a smacked bottom if you're not careful,' said Dad. 'Now behave.'

At least Meryl and Mandy and Mona cheered up a little to see Daddy's little darling getting told off for once.

Even Micky managed a watery little smile – but

49

he couldn't obey Dad and enjoy himself. The food in the Copper Kettle was delicious but Micky could only manage a few mouthfuls. Even his creamy mashed potato could barely slip past the lump in his throat

'You won't get any pudding if you don't finish your first course,' said Dad.

Micky didn't care. He watched the rest of the family scooping their way through giant ice-cream sundaes without a flicker of interest.

'Yum yum, that was lovely grub,' said Dad. He peered out of the window. 'And I do believe the rain's clearing up. So. What shall we all do this afternoon?'

'Well, I'd like to go round the shops – only there aren't any decent ones,' said Meryl.

'I'd like to go to the sports centre and try out the facilities – but I don't think there's one of them either,' said Mandy.

'I'd like to go to the amusement arcade – but where *is* it?' said Mona, sighing theatrically.

'Micky? Where would you like to go, son?' said Dad, trying to make friends with him.

Micky shrugged. 'I don't know,' he mumbled. He did know of course. He wanted to go straight back to Wolfie.

'*I* know where *I* want to go,' said Marigold. 'I want to go on the pier. There *is* a pier, I know, I saw it.'

'What a good idea,' said Dad heartily, ruffling Marigold's curls.

The pier was Victorian, with a creaking turnstile and wooden planks that didn't always fit edge to edge, so you could peep through to the green sea churning underneath. It made Micky's stomach churn a little too and Marigold refused to step on any crack, which made her walk very oddly indeed.

'Let me be the Mac-Monster again, Dad,' she said, but it had stopped raining at last and Dad had folded his mac away.

'Then give me a piggy-back, Dad,' said Marigold.

Dad carried her a few yards, even neighing obligingly like a horse, but Marigold was a solid little girl and Dad soon started sagging.

'You'll have to get down now, sweetheart, I'm getting worn out,' said Dad.

Marigold slid down ungraciously and picked her way over the planks, stepping high as if scared the waves could suck her through the cracks.

'I don't like this pier,' she said.

But the others were starting to have fun. Granny Boot went on the Bingo stall and won two teddies, a miniature teapot and a purple troll in no time. Mum went to have her palm read by the fortune teller and came back, cheeks flushed, muttering about romantic holiday adventures.

'I'll be your romantic holiday adventure,' said Dad, and he bought her a bunch of pink plastic roses from the gift boutique.

Meryl spent ages inside a booth selling postcards and pop posters because there was a group of

Italian language students squashed inside too, most of them boys.

Mandy went right to the end of the pier and got chatting to the fishermen, trying to talk them into liberating their fish like a true vegetarian.

Mona spent all her holiday pocket money trying to win a rainbow panda out of the cranes. The rainbow panda remained firmly wedged into place, but she managed to win a turquoise mouse and a yellow hippo instead.

Micky mooched off down the pier by himself. There was a plump man with a beard painting a picture of the sea front. Micky stood watching him for a while.

'Do you like painting?' said the man.

'Mmm,' said Micky.

He didn't feel up to conversation. The artist seemed to understand. He got on with his painting, giving happy little sighs as he dabbed and daubed. His painting was very happy too, much brighter and bluer and bolder than the real scene.

'It reflects my mood, you see,' he said, as if Micky had made a comment.

'Mmm,' said Micky.

If he'd had his crayons and sketch book with him he'd only need one colour to reflect *his* mood. Black.

He couldn't cheer up at all, even when the sun came out and they went on the sands and played French cricket and then had fish and chips for tea. Even Granny Boot got a little exasperated with Micky's gloom and despair.

'How many more times do I have to tell you, ducks? Wolfie will have settled in nicely now. He'll be all tucked up with his blanket and his bone, enjoying his own little holiday.'

'Yes, but what if . . . ' Micky's face screwed up with anxiety. 'I'm so scared he might have managed to escape, you see, you know how good he is at doing that. And then, if he's lost . . . '

'How about phoning the dog shelter then, just to put your mind at rest?' Granny suggested.

Dad wouldn't hear of it. He said Micky was to put Wolfie right out of his mind.

Micky was going out of his mind with worry thinking of Wolfie. He couldn't get to sleep at all when he went to bed. Marigold cuddled down straight away, and Granny Boot soon started dozing over her blockbuster and settled down, snoring softly.

Micky tossed and turned, unable to get comfy, his sheets tangled, his pillow soggy with his secret tears. The weather outside seemed to be matching his mood, raining again. It was very windy too, the trees rustling eerily outside. The old Amber Hotel creaked and groaned, the wind whistling down the chimneys, and something started howling outside, wanting to be let in.

Something started howling . . .

Micky sat bolt upright in bed. Those howls were wonderfully familiar!

6 . . .

'Wolfie!' Micky gasped.

The howls became deafening and insistent. There was no mistake. It really was Wolfie. And if Micky didn't do something about him he was going to wake the whole hotel.

Micky shot out of bed. The room was dark and he wasn't quite sure where everything was. He stepped on something warm and furry and gave a little squeak of astonishment, but it was only one of Granny Boot's bedroom slippers.

She was snoring in earnest now, her lips smacking as if she were having a private midnight snack. Granny seemed unlikely to wake even if Wolfie howled right in her ear – but Marigold was a different matter. She was stirring restlessly already, and when Micky opened the bedroom door she called out.

'Micky? Where you going?' she mumbled, still half asleep.

'Just nipping to the toilet. Go back to sleep,' Micky whispered, praying that Wolfie wouldn't howl again and wake her properly.

It was as if Wolfie somehow understood, because he was suddenly silent. Micky hurried off down the corridor towards the stairs, hoping that Marigold would snuggle down again. He held his breath as he went past Mum and Dad's door, but their room seemed dark and silent. There was a gleam of light under Meryl and Mandy and Mona's door, and muffled giggling, but at least they didn't seem bothered about what might be happening outside.

Wolfie was howling again, his voice high-pitched, getting desperate.

'I'm coming, Wolfie, I'm coming,' Micky gabbled, hurtling down the stairs.

The front door was locked up for the night and it took Micky ages tugging and pulling at the heavy bolts. He heard Wolfie scrabbling and whimpering outside, as if he was trying to help. Micky couldn't possibly reach the top bolt and had to run off in search of a chair to stand on – and even then it was such a stretch that Micky overbalanced and

toppled forward, landing painfully on his hands and knees. But he was up again in a minute and having another go, though he kept looking over his shoulder anxiously in case the owners of the hotel should hear him and think him a burglar.

The top bolt was so stiff that at first it wouldn't budge, but when Micky yanked it desperately, scratching all his fingers, it suddenly gave way and slid open. Then Micky tumbled down off the chair, pulled the door open at long last, rushed out on to the gravel pathway – and into the huge hairy embrace of his frantic best friend.

'Oh Wolfie Wolfie Wolfie,' Micky whispered, overcome.

Wolfie panted ecstatically, licking Micky all over. His lick was extra sticky and when Micky peered at him in the porch light he saw they were both now smeared with something dark.

'Chocolate,' said Micky, wiping at the matted hairs around Wolfie's mouth. 'Oh you ever so clever boy. You found all the chocolates I threw out of the car for you. I so hoped you'd be able to follow me that way. And yet I was so scared you'd get lost. How did you ever escape in the first place?'

Wolfie threw his head in the air and snuffled contemptuously. This was obviously werepuppy language for 'easy peasy'.

'But it was such a long long way for you to come too,' said Micky. 'I didn't realize just how long a journey it would be. You must be so tired now – and your poor old paws must be so sore.'

Micky gently lifted Wolfie's legs, trying to examine the pads of his paws. Wolfie winced a little, wriggling. He gave a haughty little howl to remind Micky that he was no ordinary pup. He was a weird and wondrous werewolf, capable of trekking night and day. But he yawned hugely in mid-howl, obviously exhausted.

'My poor boy, you're so sleepy,' said Micky. 'Where can we tuck you up, eh?' He peered round the dark sodden garden.

Wolfie scrabbled indignantly at Micky's pyjama jacket.

'No, Wolfie, you can't come in my bed,' said Micky. 'Maybe Granny would cover up for us, but we're sharing with Marigold, and you know what *she's* like.'

Wolfie growled in agreement.

'Yes, she'd tell Dad and then he'd pack you off back to the dog shelter all over again,' said Micky.

Wolfie shivered.

'Don't worry, though, Wolfie, I'll find you somewhere safe,' said Micky. 'Come on, boy.'

Wolfie sprang to attention, but limped a little.

'Here, I'll carry you,' said Micky, scooping him up in his arms.

Now it was Micky's turn to stagger, because Wolfie was growing rapidly every day and now weighed almost as much as his master. But Micky was filled with so much love and pride for his faithful pet that he'd have happily hauled him along if he was twice the size. Wolfie laid his large head on Micky's shoulder, his amber eyes already starting to droop.

'So where can we bed you down for the night, eh?' Micky said, stumbling about the gardens with his big burden of snoozing werepuppy.

There were hedges and shrubs, but they were nowhere big enough to hide Wolfie. There were big wooden barrels Wolfie might just have fitted inside but they were all planted with flowers. Micky made his way to the children's play area right at the bottom of the garden. He sat down heavily on the wet swing, balancing Wolfie carefully over his knees. Then he saw the perfect holiday hidey-home for Wolfie. It was a large pink plastic playhouse, big enough for a girl Marigold's size to stand up in.

Micky slung his slumbering great pup over his shoulder and staggered off the swing over to the playhouse. He got the door open and with great difficulty stuffed Wolfie inside. Wolfie woke up while this was going on and grumbled.

'Hey, don't you growl at me, boy,' said Micky, sticking his head through the door. 'There now. Comfy?'

Wolfie certainly seemed comfortable enough. There was some doll's furniture and a tea-set and a teddy or two, but Wolfie swept them aside with one flick of his tail, clearing his own space.

'That's right, boy. Now, you settle down,' said Micky.

He gave Wolfie a good-night hug and kiss, reaching right into the house so that his bottom stuck up

in the air. Then he tried to wriggle away, but Wolfie started to howl as he withdrew.

'Sh! Don't start howling again. You've got to stay hidden, Wolfie.'

Wolfie whimpered, obviously not ready to be parted from Micky all over again.

'I know, Wolfie, I know,' said Micky, giving him another big hug. He wondered about squeezing right into the playhouse and spending the whole night with Wolfie – but it was much too risky. Marigold might well still be awake. If he didn't get back soon she might send out the alarm. Micky could sense her tick-tocking away, getting ready to shriek.

'I'll *have* to go back to bed, Wolfie. You snuggle up and go to sleep, boy.' Micky tried to sound firm. Wolfie was not impressed. He started a high-pitched keening sound, trying to hang on to Micky with his sore paws.

'Let me *go*, Wolfie,' said Micky.

Wolfie hung on grimly, taking a large portion of Micky's pyjama jacket in his teeth as a precaution.

'Hey, you have the rest of my jacket too. It can be instead of your blanket. OK?'

Wolfie wasn't particularly impressed by this idea. He wanted the whole of Micky, or at the very least the whole of his pyjamas. When Micky had struggled out of his jacket Wolfie snapped softly at his pyjama bottoms, trying to pull them off too.

'Give over, Wolfie!' said Micky, giggling. 'Come on now, settle down.'

Wolfie sighed sulkily, but snuffled into Micky's pyjama jacket, using it like a cuddle blanket.

'That's right. Good boy. Night night now. And I'll whiz back to see you first thing tomorrow.'

Micky backed out of the playhouse and crept back across the garden, tiptoeing painfully along the gravel path. Wolfie whimpered once or twice. When the moon came out from behind the clouds he gave one last howl – but then he was quiet.

Micky's heart started thumping painfully when he got to the front door because it looked as if it might have blown shut – but it was simply resting

on the latch. Micky got inside and managed to get it bolted back into place. He realized he was now sopping wet, and his bare feet were very muddy. He didn't want to leave a track of dirty footprints, so with immense presence of mind he pulled his pyjama trousers down over his feet and knotted the ends. He had to hobble back up the stairs, clutching at the waistband to keep himself decently covered.

Marigold had gone back to sleep, but she woke again as Micky blundered round her bed.

'Where have you *been*?'

'The toilet. Told you,' Micky whispered.

'But that was ages ago, wasn't it?'

'No. Go back to sleep,' said Micky.

'Why are you walking all funny?' said Marigold.

'I'm not,' said Micky, jumping into bed. 'Now go to *sleep*.'

Luckily Marigold did just that. And Micky cuddled up too, cold without his pyjama jacket, uncomfortably wet and muddy around his legs, but blissfully happy that Wolfie was only just outside in his newly appropriated pastel pink kennel.

7 . . .

Micky crept out very early the next morning, wisely discarding his pyjama trousers and pulling on shorts and plimsolls. The hotel landlady was up before him and had unbolted the front door.

'You're an early bird,' she said to Micky. 'I haven't started the breakfasts yet.'

'Oh, it's OK. I'm just going to have a little walk, that's all,' said Micky.

'There's a swing at the end of the garden,' said the hotel landlady. 'And there's a playhouse too – though you're probably a bit big for that.'

'Probably,' said Micky, running outside.

There was no room for any child in the playhouse now, big or little. A tip of grey tail stuck out of one window, and a paw poked out of the door. There was a gentle snoring sound from within.

Micky hoped there weren't any small children staying at the Amber Hotel. They might well get quite a shock if they tried to toddle through the little door into the pink playhouse. Still, at least Wolfie was quiet now. It looked as if he'd be safely asleep for a long time yet.

Marigold and Granny Boot were getting dressed when Micky got back to the bedroom.

'Where were you *this* time?' Marigold asked.

'Toilet,' said Micky.

'Again?' said Marigold. 'You kept on going to the toilet in the night, didn't you?'

'Yes, well, I've got this tummy upset, see,' said Micky.

'Have you, dear?' said Granny, concerned. 'You should have woken me up. Dear oh dear, it was obviously all those chocolate toffees. And getting all worked up and in a state about Wolfie. Tell you what, Micky. We'll slope off after breakfast, just you and me, and we'll phone up the dog shelter to put your mind at rest. Your dad need never know.'

'Oh, it's OK, Granny, really,' said Micky hastily. 'I'm sure Wolfie's fine now.'

Granny Boot looked at him, astonished. Even Marigold's mouth gaped open.

'And I'm fine too,' said Micky firmly. 'I'm going to enjoy my holiday now, you'll see.'

Everyone remarked on the new changed cheery Micky at breakfast.

'Gran says you had a bit of a tummy upset in the night,' said Mum. 'You're better now, Micky? You're certainly tucking into your breakfast with a good appetite. Fancy you eating all those sausages!'

'I like sausages,' said Micky. He looked at Meryl's plate. 'They're very very fattening though.'

Meryl looked alarmed and put her knife and fork down at once.

'I'll eat yours for you,' said Micky, scraping them off her plate. He scraped them off his own plate too, when no one was looking. His shorts

pockets were full to bursting now with a very good breakfast for Wolfie.

'It looks as if it's actually going to be a sunny day,' said Dad chirpily. 'Who fancies a game of French cricket on the sands?'

'I'll sit in a deck-chair and watch,' said Mum. 'Yes, that storm last night certainly cleared the air. Did it wake any of you up? The wind was really *howling*.'

Micky had a sudden coughing fit. Granny Boot banged him hard on the back.

'Did a sausage go down the wrong way? You really shouldn't bolt your food like that, lovey, especially if your tummy's a bit upset.'

'No, I'm fine, Gran, really,' said Micky, spluttering.

'So you'll come and play French cricket, son?' said Dad.

'Er . . . well, maybe I'd better hang around the hotel a bit this morning, just in case my tummy starts up again,' said Micky quickly. He was pretty useless at most sports and Dad tended to shout at him if he missed the ball.

'I'll play cricket with you, Dad,' said Mandy.

'I will too – and I'm going in swimming,' said Mona.

'Yes, do you think it's warm enough to wear a bikini?' said Meryl, who had no serious swimming plans but wanted to show herself off to any passing language students.

'What about you, Marigold?' said Dad fondly, as his youngest child galloped her Little Ponies round her cornflakes plate and up and over her mug of milk.

'I want to play in the garden here. The lady says they've got a special playhouse,' she said.

'Oh, that's just for babies,' said Micky hurriedly. 'You don't want to hang around there, Marigold. Why don't you take all your ponies down on the beach, and if I'm feeling better later on then I'll come and build you a riding stable out of sand, and we can make them a special gymkhana field with lolly sticks for jumps.'

Marigold looked at Micky suspiciously. She couldn't understand why he was suddenly being so helpful at providing holiday stabling for her Little Ponies, but he was very clever at making things, so she decided to take him up on this – and mercifully forgot all about the playhouse.

Granny Boot volunteered to look after Micky while the rest of the family went to the beach. While Granny was fetching her cardi Micky raced to check up on Wolfie. He was still fast asleep, although he snuffled appreciatively when Micky poked a hand through the window to give him a pat.

'That's it, boy. You have a nice long rest,' Micky whispered.

'Hey, is that why you put Marigold off? Do you want to play in the dinky little house yourself?' Granny said, trotting down the path and smiling at him.

'Oh! No, catch me playing in a baby house like that,' Micky said quickly, backing away.

Bits of Wolfie were still sticking out of the windows and door but Granny was short-sighted, so he hoped she wouldn't spot anything amiss.

'I checked up with the hotel landlady – there's a car boot sale today, up on top of the cliffs. Fancy going to it in an hour or so, if your tum's quietened down?' said Granny.

'It's quiet now, honestly,' said Micky. 'I'd love to go.'

When Granny Boot's back was turned he dug in his pockets for squashed sausages and hastily dropped them down the chimney. If Wolfie woke he'd be surrounded by his favourite breakfast, so he should be happy enough.

Micky and Granny set off to the boot sale. It was a very big crowded affair, and Granny started darting around the stalls, seizing on all sorts of bargains for her shop back at home. Micky ambled along after her. He wasn't very interested in old clothes but he liked rootling amongst the toys and ornaments. He'd started to collect a series of small china animals called Whimsies. They were mostly only about fifty pence, and Granny Boot often helped him out if he didn't have enough pocket money. He had a little Whimsie dog, but Granny had told him she was sure there was a special Whimsie wolf. Micky squinted hopefully at each fresh stall, looking for a tiny china Wolfie. He had to dodge and dive a bit, because he was little and skinny and lots of people pushed past him. Micky timidly tried some push and shove tactics of his own.

'Here, what are you playing at, mate?'

'Who are you shoving, you snotty-nosed little twit?'

Micky had accidentally bumped into two tall heavy metal fans flicking their way through a box of bootleg CDs. One had Guns'n'Roses on his T-shirt, the other Iron Maiden. They didn't look remotely rosy or maidenly.

'Sorry,' said Micky hastily.

Unfortunately Granny Boot chose to shout and wave to him at that exact moment.

'Cooeee!' Granny trilled. 'Over here, pet! Whimsies!'

Guns'n'Roses and Iron Maiden cracked up.

'Whimsies! Is that the little berk's *name*?'

'Go on, Whimsie-Mimsie-Pimsie, that daft old bat's calling you.'

Micky swallowed hard.

'She's not a daft old bat,' he said shakily. 'She's my gran.'

'Well, she looks pretty daft to me, and she's certainly old, and she's flapping her arms around at you like a bat,' said Guns'n'Roses.

'Cooooeeeee,' shrieked Iron Maiden, doing a very unkind imitation of Granny Boot.

'You cut that out,' said Micky, trying to sound stern and resolute.

It made them laugh harder than ever.

'Hark at little Whimsie here!'

'Going to clock us one, are you?'

They started jostling Micky, their big hot hands on his shoulders.

'Micky?' Granny Boot had seen what was going on. 'Come over here.'

'Go on, little Whimsie, batty old Granny wants you.'

'Yes, she doesn't want you to play wiv us wough boys,' said Guns'n'Roses, putting on a silly accent.

'Oh-oh, she's coming over here. Oooh, will she spank us?' said Iron Maiden, sounding equally silly.

'What are you two louts doing to my grandson?' Granny Boot demanded, rushing up. 'Take your hands off him.'

Guns'n'Roses and Iron Maiden cackled with laughter.

'Ah, shut up, you daft old bat,' said Guns'n'Roses.

'Yeah, bog off,' said Iron Maiden.

'Don't you dare talk to my gran like that,' Micky shouted, red-hot with rage, so angry now that he forgot to be scared. He itched all over and there was a roaring in his head that got louder and louder. There was a snarl and a growl and Micky wondered if they were coming from his own lips. But he was gently nudged aside by a familiar grey friend, grown huge and fierce and ferocious.

Wolfie leapt up at Guns'n'Roses and Iron Maiden and they started yelling like a heavy metal band themselves. They turned and ran, which was a mistake. Wolfie saw two denim bottoms and decided he wanted a bit of fun. He leapt up and gave their jeans several interesting new designer slashes. Guns'n'Roses and Iron Maiden ran on, shrieking.

'Help, there's a mad dog on the loose!' people yelled.

'It's not a mad dog, it's just my puppy,' said Micky. 'Here, Wolfie!'

Wolfie decided to be obedient for once. Perhaps he'd had enough fun already. He happily skidded to a halt, gave one small snort at the retreating boys, and then trotted back to Micky and Granny Boot.

'Well I never!' said Granny, shaking her head. 'So where on earth did you spring from, young Wolfie?'

'Did I wake you up when I posted those sausages down the chimney?' said Micky, hugging Wolfie happily.

Wolfie had smelt the hot dog stall and was sniffing the air urgently, demanding another breakfast immediately.

Granny Boot sportingly bought them all a hot dog, and while they munched Micky explained about Wolfie's Tremendous Trek.

'You will help me keep him hidden from the others, won't you, Gran?' said Micky. 'I *can't* send him back now when he's been so clever to find me.'

'Well, I don't know *how* we're going to keep him hidden – but I'll do my best to help,' Granny promised.

At Sunday lunch Granny seemed to demolish her plate of roast beef almost at one gulp. She asked for a second serving.

'The sea air's certainly done you a lot of good, Mum,' said Micky's mum. 'You've really got your appetite back.'

'That's not all we've got back, eh, Micky?' Granny whispered, secretly showing him the roast beef she'd tucked into her handbag for a special Wolfie snack.

8 . . .

It was an almost impossible task keeping Wolfie hidden away, out of sight. Once he was fully recovered from his long tiring trek he didn't want to be stuffed back into the pink playhouse. He wanted to be up and doing. He especially wanted to be out on the prowl at night, like any normal werepuppy with a full-moon gleam in his golden eyes.

'You must try to be *good*, Wolfie,' Micky said, wishing he could risk taking the puppy to sleep in his hotel bedroom, where he could keep a proper eye on him. But if Marigold got one little whiff of Wolfie then she'd blab straight to Dad.

So Wolfie spent the night outside – and didn't spend much time in the playhouse. The next morning there were many wrecked gardens in the little seaside town, and a long queue of pet-owners outside the veterinary surgery, clutching traumatized cats and terrorized dogs.

The guests in the hotel started talking about strange howlings and growlings that had woken them in the night. Micky started fidgeting anxiously but Granny Boot developed a sudden and spectacular coughing fit that diverted everyone's attention.

'Oh dear, Mum, I thought you were completely over that bronchitis,' said Micky's mum anxiously.

'I think I need a long walk along the cliffs to get some sea air,' Granny spluttered. 'You'll keep your old gran company, won't you, Micky?'

They managed to get away from the others and sneak Wolfie out of his temporary kennel.

'Though you obviously weren't in it much last night!' said Micky sternly. 'What am I going to *do* with you, Wolfie?'

Micky and Granny took Wolfie for a very long walk, hoping to tire him out. Wolfie didn't tire a bit, even though he'd been up all night. Micky tired a little and poor Granny Boot tired a lot. She had to have a long nap after lunch. Micky tried to stay with her but Mum wouldn't hear of it. He was forced to join the rest of the family on the beach.

Wolfie had to be left to his own devices. Micky worried a great deal, wondering what on earth he

was up to. He also worried on his own behalf because Dad wouldn't just let him mooch about the beach doing his own thing. He had to join in all the silly ball games even though Micky always managed to miss the ball completely. Everyone got very hot running around in the sunshine. Dad got red in the face shouting at Micky to keep his eye on the ball. Micky burned all over because everyone on the beach seemed to be looking at him.

It was almost a relief when Marigold reminded him that he'd promised to make her some sand stables for her Little Pony. Micky set to work with a spade and had soon built her an elaborate pony palace with separate shell-studded individual stalls and a practice paddock.

The artist who'd been painting on the pier came strolling along the sands and stopped to admire Micky's efforts.

'Gosh, that's really great,' he said, shaking his head admiringly.

Dad came panting up, trying to catch a ball that Mandy had hit for six. He was running sideways, keeping his eye on the ball so steadily that he couldn't see what his feet were doing.

'Hey, watch out!' shouted the artist, but it was too late.

Dad's feet bulldozed half the pony palace, and caused a minor earthquake in the seaweed ornamental gardens.

'Dad, you've wrecked my palace!' Marigold yelled.

'Oh dear. I'm sorry, love,' said Dad. 'Sorry, Micky. Still, you can make another sand-castle, can't you?'

'He's very good at sand modelling,' said the artist quietly. 'You've got a very talented son.'

Dad looked astonished. But pleased. Maybe Micky's hands were useless when it came to catching balls but they could also be clever at making castles.

'Yes, he's a good lad,' said Dad, ruffling Micky's hair.

The artist smiled and gave Micky a wink when Dad wasn't looking. Micky winked back and then cheerily started rebuilding the shattered sand palace. He almost started to enjoy himself, although his ears were still pricked on red alert for distant howls.

Granny came on the beach after her nap.

'Did you see Wolfie?' Micky whispered. 'Is he staying hidden in the pink playhouse?'

'Not exactly,' said Granny. 'When I went to check up on him he was having the time of his life playing catch-the-towel with the hotel's washing line. I went after him but he was off like a grey streak. The towels have got a few grey streaks too, I'm afraid.'

Micky started worrying again, getting hot and bothered.

'Let's go in swimming,' said Mona, wanting to show off her new talent.

'Good idea. Off you go, all of you,' said Mum. 'I'll watch the bags.' She smoothed sun-tan oil on herself and settled back on the sand, a smile on her face.

Granny was game for a paddle though, wriggling out of her tights as coyly as she could and then splashing through the shallows. Micky and Marigold played either side of her, while Mona and Mandy swam properly and Meryl stood posing in her bikini at the water's edge. She was soon surrounded by eager language students who enticed her away to play quoits with them.

Dad wasn't too happy about this, but there wasn't much he could do about it. He decided to concentrate on the rest of his family. He made a fuss of Mona because she could swim so well. Mandy could swim well too, and was paddling around on a piece of board, trying to do a spot of improvised surf riding.

'So how about you lot coming in further than your kneecaps?' said Dad eagerly, addressing the paddlers.

'If I tuck my frock up any higher I'll be showing my knickers,' said Granny Boot.

'I meant Micky and Marigold,' said Dad. 'Come on, kids, it's time you learnt to swim properly.'

Micky sighed and started shivering in spite of the hot sun. Why did Dad always want to do things *properly*?

Dad forced Micky and Marigold to wade in further up to their waists. He tried to encourage them to duck down to get used to the water.

'My bottom bit isn't quite used to the water yet, so my top bit wants to stay warm and dry just for the moment,' said Marigold, who wasn't at all sure she wanted to learn to swim either.

Dad showed them how to push out with their arms and kick with their legs. He shouted 'One two three, one two three,' while they did their best to copy his actions out of the water, feeling foolish.

'Now let's try it for real. Don't worry, I'll hold you up,' said Dad. 'Who's going to go first?'

Micky and Marigold fought to go second.

'Oh, why don't you leave the kiddies be?' said Granny. 'They'll swim in their own good time, just like our Mona. It seems daft to force them when they just want to have fun.' She splashed her feet a little. Some of the splash went straight in Dad's face.

Dad went rather red.

'Swimming is fun,' he said shortly. 'Come on, Micky. Let's show your gran, eh, son?' Dad waved his arms about as he spoke. The waving sprayed water. Quite a lot of the spray soaked Gran's frock.

Gran retreated. Micky had to advance.

'Now, Micky, I'll put my hand under your chin like this, to keep it well out of the water – and my other hand will be under your waist, so you can't possibly sink. Right? So all you've got to do is push with your arms and kick with your legs and then you'll be swimming.'

Dad made it sound reasonably simple. It didn't work that way. Micky pushed and kicked frantically, but Dad's hand under his chin didn't stop the water sploshing straight in his face and making him splutter. He stopped pushing and kicking.

'Come on, son, swim,' Dad said, trying to push him upwards.

Micky opened his mouth to tell Dad he didn't want to swim any more. It was a mistake. He drank a huge mouthful of salty sea water and spouted it out like a whale, coughing and choking.

'For goodness sake, you're drowning him,' said Granny, wading right in and getting her frock wet.

She caught hold of Micky and plucked him out.

Dad snorted in disgust. This made Marigold suddenly determined.

'*I'll* have a go at swimming, Dad,' she said. 'I'm not a silly scaredy-cat like Micky.'

'That's my girl,' said Dad delightedly. 'Come on then, pet. Push and kick, right? I won't let you go, I promise.'

Granny and Micky retreated back up the beach to where Mum lay sleeping.

'Here, you're shivering fit to bust. Let's get you dry, ducks,' said Granny, wrapping Micky in a big towel. 'Where's my hanky? You need to blow your nose.'

'I've blown it with Dad,' Micky spluttered sadly. 'I wish I *could* learn to swim.'

Mandy came running out of the sea to get Granny to dig a splinter out of her finger.

'I'll teach you to swim, Micky,' she said. 'Come on, we'll go over the rocks round to the next bay, right away from Dad.'

'I don't think I like swimming,' said Micky, but he went off arm in arm with Mandy, while Granny settled down on the sands, spreading out her skirts to dry.

The next bay was rather small and rocky and almost deserted, which was a relief. Micky didn't want another audience. There was only one other swimmer in the sea. He was a strong swimmer, too, although his strokes weren't very stylish. He didn't do breast-stroke or freestyle. He did doggy-paddle.

'I don't believe it!' said Mandy, blinking in the bright sunshine and squinting out to sea. 'Isn't that *Wolfie?*'

'Mmm, I think it might be,' Micky agreed. 'I didn't know Wolfie could swim.'

'I didn't know Wolfie was *here*,' said Mandy.

Wolfie barked joyfully at the sight of them and came ploughing through the waves. He bounded up to Micky and shook himself vigorously, so that it suddenly seemed to be raining heavily.

'Shoo, Wolfie, you're soaking me,' said Micky.

Wolfie seemed to think that if Micky was wet he might just as well come in the water. He nudged at

Micky's knees, pushing him gently but firmly into the shallows. He barked once or twice, as if telling him what to do.

'Micky, how come Wolfie's here on holiday?' said Mandy, but she soon saw it was time for a swimming lesson, not a long boring explanation.

Wolfie took it upon himself to be the main swimming instructor. He didn't care about pushing and kicking and doing it properly. He just hurled himself into the water and waggled all four paws at once. He managed perfectly.

He barked at Micky, telling him to have a go too.

Micky was careful to stay in very shallow water, with Mandy hovering just in case. He hurled himself forwards. His head went under – but his arms and legs scrabbled. His head came up. His arms and legs went on scrabbling.

'I'm swimming!' he shouted.

It was a mistake. He took another great gulp of salty water.

But he'd still swum several strokes all the same. And with Wolfie and Mandy's encouragement he tried again and again and swam several more. Then Wolfie ran off up the beach and Micky and Mandy went over the rocks round the bay to show Dad that Micky could swim after all.

Marigold could only do one stroke, and that was with one foot on the ground.

Micky could do six strokes all by himself.

Granny Boot and Mum sat up and cheered him, and Dad said he'd make a real swimmer of him yet.

9 . . .

Now that Mandy knew about Wolfie too it made things a little easier. Mum and Dad were used to her wandering off by herself, so she could take Wolfie for long secret walks. She tried fashioning him a makeshift lead from Marigold's skipping rope, but Wolfie was a dab paw at ducking his head and escaping whenever he wanted. He frequently fancied a dip in the sea – and on one of these impromptu dips he swam out round the bay, dived under a floating tangle of seaweed, and surfaced nose to nose with Mona.

She shrieked, understandably startled by this shaggy grey creature with seaweed trailing from its snout. Wolfie snuffled and woofed to show her he was no sea-monster from the deep, and then swam companionably by her side for a few minutes before doggy-paddling back around the bay. Mona followed – and saw Mandy wading through the shallows shouting to Wolfie to come back.

So now Mona was in on the Wolfie secret too – and then Meryl came back from a sunset beach disco telling her sisters about this wild dog that streaked along the sands and snatched half the steaks from the barbecue.

'I know it sounds crazy but he was the spitting

image of Wolfie,' said Meryl. 'I called him and he looked round at me. You know that way he's got of cocking his head to one side. Even though he had a mouth full of stolen steak he still managed to grin at me – but then he ran off before I could catch him. *Could* it have been Wolfie, do you think?'

'We don't think,' said Mandy, grinning.

'We *know*,' said Mona, giggling.

Mum was the next to find out. When the rest of the family went on the sands she hung back, stopping to chat to the artist at the end of the pier.

'You were admiring my son's sand-castle the other day,' Mum said. 'Do you really think he's got artistic ability?'

'Yes, I think he's a very talented lad,' said the artist.

'Well, certainly his school teacher did tell us he'd done some lovely paintings that she'd put up on the wall,' Mum said happily. 'I wonder if he'll grow up to be a proper artist like you? I do love the way you've done that beach scene. I like the little humorous touches – especially that naughty dog running away with the towel just as that gentleman is changing into his swimming trunks!'

'That really happened,' said the artist, chuckling. 'That dog's a real character. I've seen it several times, and it's always getting into mischief.'

'We've got a dog just like that at home,' said Mum. Then she looked more closely at the painting. 'In fact we've got a dog *exactly* like that.'

Mum said nothing more – but she took careful note of the fact that one or other member of her family were frequently disappearing. She watched out at mealtimes and saw that three of her daughters, her son, and indeed her mother were all surreptitiously stowing part of their meal into their laps, pockets and handbag. She saw scratches on her children's legs and curly grey hairs decorating her mother's cardigan. She heard several trips up and down the stairs at night, and distant howling. Mum saw, Mum heard, but she said nothing.

Dad didn't need to know. He was so happy and peaceful and relaxed. It would be such a shame to spoil his holiday.

Marigold would normally have sensed a secret by now, but she had made friends with a whole gaggle of little girls that she met on the beach every day, and she was so busy giggling with them all the time that she hardly spent a minute with the family. They were all looking forward to the special seaside festival fête on Friday. There was going to be a fancy dress competition and a talent contest. Marigold was determined to win both. So were all her friends. They all wanted to dress up as princesses or pop stars and they all wanted to sing and dance in the talent contest. A whole troupe of plump ungainly little girls pranced up and down the sands, singing their hearts out.

'For pity's sake, Marigold, give it a rest!' Dad begged, trying to have a little snooze in his deck-chair.

But Mum and Gran had decided there was no reason why they couldn't go in for the talent contest too, so they started practising a souped-up version of 'How Much is that Doggy in the Window'.

Meryl and Mandy and Mona decided to try a little number of their own, and came up with a very rock'n'roll raucous version of 'Hound Dog'.

Dad couldn't work out why most of his women-folk seemed obsessed with doggy themes, and he didn't appreciate any of their acts.

'Pipe down the lot of you!' Dad begged. 'Can't a man get a bit of peace for five minutes?' He caught Micky's eye and sighed. 'Women!'

'Yeah, Dad. Women,' Micky agreed, wishing they'd all stop nudging each other and giggling whenever they sang the word dog, just in case Dad cottoned on. Micky decided he had too much on his plate trying to keep tabs on Wolfie to go in for the talent contest himself, and he certainly didn't care for the dress idea, fancy or otherwise. He'd seen on a poster that there was also a dog obedience competition at the fête, but he knew there wasn't much point entering Wolfie.

Micky chuckled at the very idea.

'You've certainly perked up a lot, son,' said Dad. 'You've had a good holiday, haven't you?'

'Mmm, yes, Dad.'

'There. I told you so. I don't want you to think I'm heartless, pal, but you can't let your life be ruled by your pets,' said Dad.

There was a faraway familiar barking.

'That's right, Dad,' said Micky. 'Er . . . I think I'll just take a little walk along the beach, OK?'

He hurried off towards the barking. Wolfie was in trouble again. He'd pounced on someone's Frisbee, mistaking it for a large white pancake. Wolfie was very partial to pancakes. There wasn't much of the Frisbee left.

'Who on earth is the owner of this wretched animal?' said the someone's dad angrily. He spotted Micky running up. 'Ah, is this your dog?' he demanded.

Micky hesitated. Wolfie caught on at once. He changed gear from welcoming barks to hostile growls, baring his teeth at Micky.

Micky acted frightened, backing away.

'*My* dog?' he said. He wasn't *exactly* telling a fib. And anyway, Wolfie wasn't a dog at all – he was a werepuppy. And he was certainly acting like it too.

Wolfie ran away, spitting out gobbets of Frisbee. Micky ran away too, in the opposite direction, but he circled round when he got to the promenade. Wolfie circled too and they met in the middle, as if they were performing an elaborate dance routine. Wolfie woofed delightedly, shards of Frisbee still in his teeth.

'No, Wolfie, you're very bad and naughty,' said Micky. 'You've got to stop getting into trouble like this.'

Wolfie put his head on one side and showed all his teeth in a challenging smile.

There was a full moon that night. Micky peered out of the window anxiously as he went to bed. He knew there was every possibility of trouble. Wolfie might very well end up having a far more sub-stantial snack than a Frisbee. He might chomp up a pet chihuahua, munch on a mongrel, gollop half a Great Dane. There was no holding him back when moon madness struck him.

'I've *got* to stop him,' Micky muttered. 'He's mine, so it's down to me.'

He parcelled up his duvet under one arm and then slyly seized Marigold's skipping rope. She was nearly nodding off to sleep – but she still saw.

'What are you doing with my skipping rope?' she demanded.

'Nothing,' said Micky, stuffing the skipping rope inside his grubby pyjama jacket. 'What skipping rope, anyway?' He unthreaded Granny's belt from her red dressing-gown, snaffled her scarf, and pulled out the cord from his anorak.

'Granny!' said Marigold, her eyes round. 'Micky's gone mad!'

'Now you settle down to sleep, pet. Granny will tell you a story. Never mind about Micky. He's off on a little errand, that's all. I daresay it's neces-sary,' said Granny Boot.

'Oh it is, Granny. Very,' said Micky.

He rushed off before Marigold could fuss further. He went out into the garden in search of Wolfie – and found him in the absolute nick of time. He was growling and slavering at the foot of a fruit tree while a terrified ginger tom teetered in the branches, emitting agonized yowls.

The cat was fat and the branch was brittle. There

88

was a snap and a mew and a bark – but just before Wolfie chewed the tom into catburger Micky pounced. He threw his duvet over Wolfie, upturned him, and wrapped him up like a giant sausage roll. Wolfie growled and howled, but Micky hung on, tying him up with all his different cords and belts. He felt inside to make sure Wolfie's head wasn't bent and his paws were quite comfy, and got badly scratched and nipped for his pains.

'You bad bad boy!' said Micky crossly. 'Look, I don't want to truss you up like this, but it's the only way we'll avoid a full-scale seaside slaughter. Stop struggling so, Wolfie! I'm not hurting you, am I?'

Micky might not want to hurt Wolfie, but Wolfie was doing his best to hurt Micky.

'Ouch!' Micky squealed, as Wolfie's snapping jaws poked out of the duvet.

He ended up tying Granny's scarf round Wolfie's head to stop him biting. He looked as if he had toothache – and howled accordingly through gritted teeth.

Granny came creeping out to see what was going on. She was ready to be cross with the pair of them but she got the giggles when she saw Wolfie.

'He looks just like the wolf pretending to be the granny in *Little Red Riding Hood*,' she spluttered. 'Oh, if only we could enter him in the fancy dress competition!'

She made Micky come back to bed once they'd both double-checked that Wolfie was safe and secure inside the duvet but Micky barely slept.

Granny Boot made him have her duvet and tucked herself up into her dressing-gown but Micky still couldn't cuddle up and get comfortable. He kept tossing and turning and twisting Granny's duvet into knots, so that he fell asleep and dreamt he was trussed up himself – and then he woke to hear Wolfie's indignant wailing outside. He must have chewed his way right through Granny's scarf.

Micky wasn't the only one Wolfie woke. Half the hotel heard the howling. Meryl and Mandy and Mona and Granny and Mum knew who was responsible. Little Marigold sat up straight in her bed and snapped her fingers. She put two and two together.

'*I* get it,' she said. 'I know who *that* is. And I bet he's been hanging around here for days. That's what they've all been going on about. Cheek! Why didn't they tell *me*? I bet Dad doesn't know. I'm going to tell.'

Marigold burst into Mum and Dad's bedroom in the morning, reading to spill the beans. But Dad was already up and downstairs. He'd had very uneasy dreams all night long.

'I kept having nightmares about that dratted dog for some unknown reason,' Dad told Mum. 'I kept dreaming that he was howling away, desperately unhappy.'

'I wonder why you dreamt that, dear?' said Mum.

'And then I couldn't get back to sleep but I was in such a state that I still thought I heard him

90

howling,' said Dad. 'Look, I think I'm going to ring that dog shelter after all. I know it's crazy, but if that wretched mutt really is pining I want to know. He drives me crazy but I'd still never forgive myself if anything happened to him. I know just how much he means to young Micky.'

'But we're going home tomorrow,' said Mum. 'There's no point phoning now.'

'No, I've simply got to put my mind at rest. Blow me, I can still hear that phantom howling now!' said Dad.

91

Down he went to phone. Then up he ran, just as Marigold was clamouring for attention.

'Not now, Marigold!' said Dad, his tanned face drained dirty yellow. 'Something terrible's happened. Wolfie's gone missing. He escaped from the shelter that very first day, and there hasn't been sight or sound of him since.'

'I think there might have been a *few* sights and sounds,' said Mum calmly.

'Dad, Dad, I know about Wolfie!' said Marigold.

'Sh, Marigold, I've got to go and find Micky and somehow break it to him. Oh dear, I feel so dreadful. He'll never trust me again,' Dad sighed.

But Micky wasn't in his bedroom.

'He's . . . busy in the garden,' said Granny Boot.

Micky was extremely busy struggling to release Wolfie from his shackled sausage. Wolfie didn't seem to bear him any grudge now the moon had disappeared. He nuzzled Micky with his bescarfed snout, giving gruff little love-woofs. Micky got the last belt untied and rolled Wolfie out of his straitjacket. Wolfie quivered, stretched, gave one joyful bark, and then bounded away.

'Hey, Wolfie! Where are you going? Come back!' Micky yelled.

In his newly freed delight Wolfie had lost all sense of direction. He was running towards the hotel. Then he smelt breakfast cooking. Bacon. Sausage. Wolfie lost all sense as well as direction. He was guided solely by his twitching nostrils. He charged kitchenwards.

'Help! Help! There's a mad dog devouring all my cooked breakfasts!' the hotel landlady shrieked.

'Wolfie!' said Micky.

'Wolfie!' said Granny Boot.

'Wolfie!' said Mum.

'Wolfie!' said Meryl.

'Wolfie!' said Mandy.

'Wolfie!' said Mona.

'Wolfie!' said Marigold.

'*Wolfie?*' said Dad.

Then Wolfie himself came rushing into the dining-room, still chomping chipolatas, and barking himself into happy hysterics at seeing his family fully assembled.

The cat was certainly out of the bag now. Well. Let's say the dog was out of the duvet.

But Dad didn't have the heart to send Wolfie home now, especially as it was right at the end of the holiday. He was so relieved that Wolfie was safe and sound that he didn't even object too much when the hotel landlady understandably asked for compensation for all her cooked breakfasts.

'So it's your dog, is it? Well, I did make it plain. We don't allow any dogs inside our hotel.'

'He's just been in the garden up till now,' said Micky. 'And he won't come in again, I promise. You're going to be as good as gold from now on, aren't you, Wolfie?'

Wolfie grinned hugely.

He was more than happy to co-operate with Granny Boot, and let her dress him up in one of her

93

nighties. Micky was much less co-operative, and objected furiously when forced into a frock of Marigold's and Granny's red dressing-gown for a hood and cloak – but he was thrilled all the same when they won first prize in the fancy dress.

Granny Boot hoped she might just score a double and win the talent contest too. She and Mum sang 'How Much is that Doggy in the Window'. They sang it very loudly, with lots of hearty hand gestures. Dad cringed in his chair, hoping that no one knew they were his relatives.

But Mum and Granny didn't win the talent contest.

Meryl and Mandy and Mona sang 'Hound Dog'. They wriggled their hips energetically like Elvis. Dad slid further down his seat, his hand over his eyes.

Meryl and Mandy and Mona didn't win the talent contest either.

Marigold and all her little girlfriends sang a selection of songs and danced until the floorboards creaked. Marigold had a habit of making up her own tunes to songs so she rarely hit the same notes as the others. Dad sat up all the same because Marigold did *look* quite cute, standing centre stage with the spotlight shining on her golden curls – but in the middle of her dance she spun round on one leg, lost her balance, and fell bump on her bottom. Dad slumped again.

Marigold and her friends didn't win the talent contest.

Micky and Wolfie won! The dog obedience competition had given Micky an idea. Wolfie came on stage first, with a dog lead tied round his front paw. Micky came trotting after him, the collar round his neck. They walked in a circle, Wolfie first, Micky scurrying by his side. Every so often Micky lagged a little. Wolfie barked – and Micky meekly came to heel, while everyone laughed.

Then Wolfie edged Micky into a corner and slipped the lead off his front paw. He jumped up at Micky to make him sit down. Then he gave one short sharp bark and walked right to the other side of the stage. Micky fidgeted and fussed until Wolfie relented and gave another bark. Micky shot across the stage and Wolfie licked him lovingly for being such an obedient boy.

Wolfie put Micky through his paces, making him fetch a banana and carry a comic and sit up and say please to get a biscuit. Wolfie forgot his act at this point and ate both banana and biscuit himself, but this just made the audience laugh harder. They clapped and roared to show their appreciation and Wolfie threw back his head and howled triumphantly, happy to be the star of the show.

'That was great, Micky! Well done, Wolfie!' Dad was sitting up proudly, shouting to show his enthusiasm.

The boy obedience act won first prize – a huge box of chocolates.

'We'll share them, Wolfie,' said Micky, opening the box to show him what it contained.

Wolfie grinned and started gulping. Wolfie didn't see the point of sharing.

'Hey, leave some for me!' Micky said, trying to snatch the box away.

Wolfie barked – and so Micky obediently let go. Wolfie rewarded him with one half-chewed soggy chocolate toffee.

It was clear who had got the upper paw.